But now Fireman Sam had to go to work. "I'll take you to the park instead," said Elvis, as they waved goodbye.

"Yes please, Elvis!" said the children. They found a good spot for a game and marked the goalposts with some clothes.

Fireman Sam

AND THE PARK GATES

by Helen Lloyd

Illustrations by The County Studio

HEINEMANN · LONDON

Fireman Sam had promised to take Norman, Sarah and James to the park to play football.

Norman was very excited and started to play.
"Norman Price is magic!" he yelled as he chased after
the ball.

He kicked the ball very hard. It flew past James the goalkeeper. "Goal! Goal!" shouted Norman.

Norman had kicked the ball so hard it shot out
through the park fence. It landed on the pavement.

He started to climb through the railings to get the ball back. "That's a very silly thing to do, Norman," called Elvis.

"The railings are very narrow. You might get stuck."
So Norman walked through the gates instead and
came back with the ball.

James and Sarah won the game, then Elvis bought everyone an ice-cream.

Dilys came to collect the three children and they went home together.

Elvis felt very tired after the game. He sat down under a shady tree and fell asleep.

Elvis was still asleep when the park closed for the night.
No-one noticed him under the tree.

Fireman Sam was waiting for Elvis to arrive for work
at the fire station.

"Where can Elvis be? He's half an hour late,"
said Fireman Sam, looking at the clock.

The village clock struck and Elvis woke up. He had to go to the fire station at once!

He walked to the park gates. They were locked now.
And they were very high. Too high to climb over.

"I'll climb through the railings," said Elvis. He forgot
what he had told Norman earlier about getting stuck.

And halfway through, Elvis did get stuck. He couldn't move backwards or forwards.

Then Elvis saw Norman and Trevor walking down the road. "Help!" shouted Elvis. "Call the Fire Brigade!"

Norman and Trevor laughed when they saw poor Elvis.
"But you are the Fire Brigade!" giggled Norman.

Trevor telephoned the fire station and spoke to
Fireman Sam. "I'll bring my cutting tools," he said.

A few minutes later, Fireman Sam arrived. Norman
and Trevor helped him, and Elvis was soon free.

Elvis felt very silly. "You must remember your own advice, Elvis!" said Fireman Sam, smiling.